The Very Best Picnic

For Marna

A GOLDEN BOOK • NEW YORK

Western Publishing Company, Inc., Racine, Wisconsin 53404

Jessie was excited. Tomorrow she was going on her very first picnic.

"I can't wait," she said to her mother. "I want to eat lunch under a tree and sail my boat on the pond. And I want to feed the baby ducks."

That night Jessie jumped right into bed. The sooner she went to sleep, the sooner it would be tomorrow.

"I hope it'll be sunny tomorrow," she said.

"Me, too," said Mother. She kissed Jessie
good night. "Sweet dreams."
Jessie closed her eyes. Soon she was fast
asleep, dreaming about the picnic.

The next morning the sun was shining. But Jessie did not get up. She felt awful.

Soon Mother came into the room. "I thought you'd be up bright and early," she said.

Jessie coughed. "I feel sleepy."

Jessie sneezed. "I feel hot."

Mother took Jessie's temperature.

Jessie had a fever. That meant no picnic. Now Jessie *really* felt awful.

Jessie pulled the covers up over her head. "I'm *never* coming out!" she said.

"Will you come out if I read you a story?" Mother asked.

"NO," said Jessie.

"Will you come out if I get you some ice cream?" Mother asked.

"NO," said Jessie.

"Ice cream with cherries on top?" said Mother.

"NO," said Jessie. "NO, NO, NO."

Mother left Jessie's room and went out to the garden. She came back with leafy branches, rocks, and flowers. She tied the branches to Jessie's bed and put the rocks and flowers on the floor.

"What are you doing?" Jessie asked.

"Come out and see for yourself," said Mother.

But Jessie did not come out.

Mother put Jessie's toy animals all around
the flowers and the rocks. Then she got the
old baby tub and filled it up with water. The
splashing water sounded strange to Jessie.

"What's that?" she asked.

"It's a beautiful little pond," said Mother, "with baby ducks swimming all around. Now will you come out?"

But Jessie did not come out.

Mother brought the picnic basket up to Jessie's room. She opened the window, and the sound of birds singing came into the room. Then Mother spread a tablecloth over Jessie's bed.

"What are you doing *now*?" Jessie asked.

"I'm having a picnic," said Mother. "Why don't you come out and join me?"

But Jessie *still* did not come out.

So Mother was *very* quiet.

Then, finally, very slowly, Jessie poked her head out from under the covers. She looked all around the room.

"Oh, Mommy," she said, "it's beautiful!"

"I'm so glad you came out," said Mother. "Now we can have our picnic. And you can feed the baby ducks."

"And I can sail my boat on the pond," said Jessie. She was very happy.

Jessie and Mother ate their picnic underneath the branches. Jessie coughed and sneezed, and she was hot. But she had a wonderful time.

"Thank you, Mommy," Jessie said. "This is the very best picnic in the whole world."